For S J J, with love ~ S C
For John King infant school and Kirkstead junior school.
Thank you for a fine education, especially the lessons
involving Plasticine and poster paints ~ S J

LITTLE TIGER PRESS LTD,
an imprint of the Little Tiger Group
1 Coda Studios
189 Munster Road
London SW6 6AW
www.littletiger.co.uk

First published in Great Britain 2018
This edition published 2019
Text by Suzanne Chiew
Text copyright © Little Tiger Press Ltd 2018
Illustrations copyright © Sean Julian 2018
Sean Julian has asserted his right to be identified
as the illustrator of this work under the Copyright,
Designs and Patents Act, 1988
A CIP catalogue record for this book
is available from the British Library

ISBN 978-1-84869-830-7
Printed in China
LTP/1400/2488/0918
10 9 8 7 6 5 4 3 2 1

The Worry Box

Suzanne Chiew   Sean Julian

LITTLE TIGER

LONDON

High up on his thinking spot, Murray Bear
looked out across the valley.
"Here you are!" called his sister, Milly.
"It's time for lunch."
"I'm not hungry," Murray sighed.
"You're always hungry!" giggled Milly.
"Come on, or we'll be late meeting
Alfie at the waterfall."

"I don't want to go!" snuffled Murray.
"What if the waterfall's too LOUD?
What if it's so BIG that I get
whooshed away?"

Milly squeezed Murray tight. "Waterfalls *are* big and loud," she said. "But they're also beautiful."

"I won't get whisked away?" asked Murray.

"Not with me to hold your paw," said Milly firmly.

Murray thought for a moment then nodded.

"Sharing worries always makes them feel smaller," Milly comforted as they headed for home.

When the very last sandwich was eaten, Milly had a secret to share.

"This is my worry box," she smiled. "When something's worrying me, I write it down, then I put it inside."

"Does it make your worries disappear?" asked Murray.

"Not quite," said Milly. "But when my worries are in the box they don't stop me having fun. Let's make one for you."

"Worries won't stop me!" cheered Murray,
popping his worry in the box and
shutting the lid tight.
    "Ready?" Milly asked.
    "Ready!" nodded Murray.

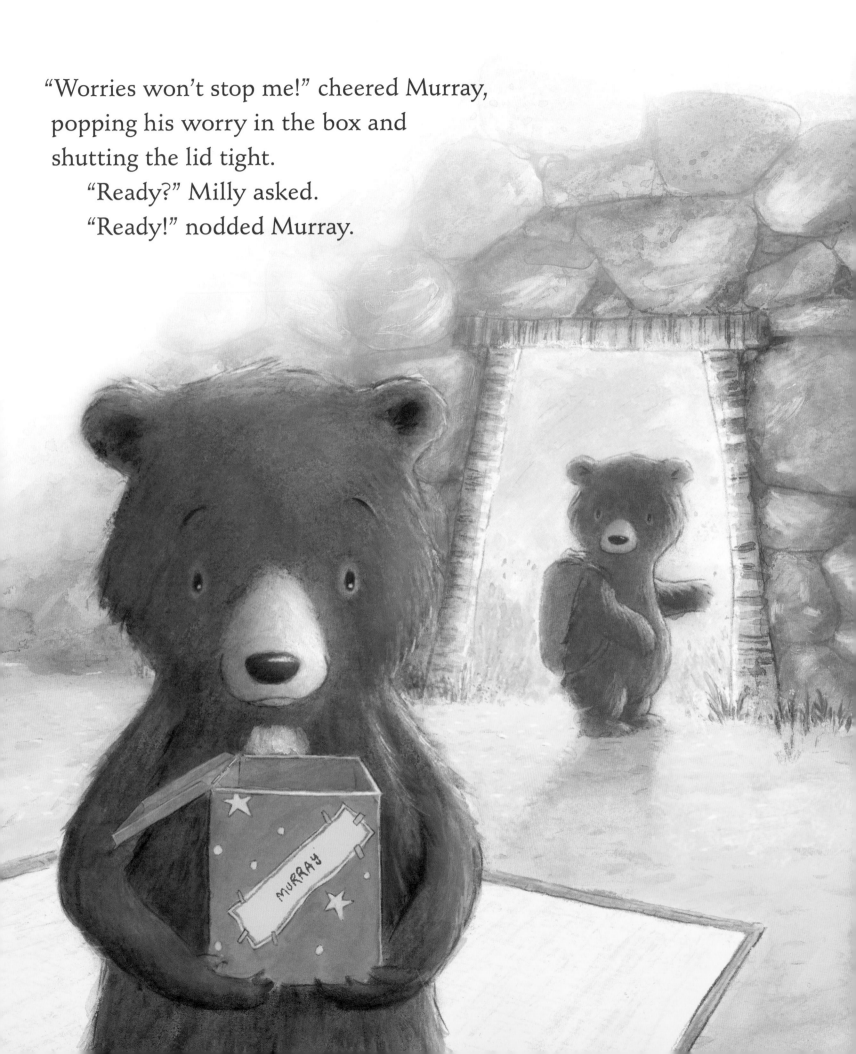

Skipping along the riverbank, the bears
spotted dragonflies dancing above
their heads.

But soon the river raced faster,
and there was a roar of water ahead.

"Nearly there," said Milly.

"Eeek," Murray squeaked
as they rounded the bend.

There, sparkling in the sunlight, was
the rumbling, tumbling waterfall.

"Wow!" gasped Murray, wiping
the spray from his nose.

Just then, there was a shout from
the rocks.

"It's Alfie!" Milly cheered.

Murray took a deep breath.
"Let's go and play," he decided.
"Last one there gets sploshed!"

The friends were busy counting
the fish when they heard a
voice calling them.

"Yoo-hoo!" cried a rabbit Murray had never met before.
"It's my cousin, Lara!" beamed Alfie.
Suddenly Murray felt very shy.

Lara scrambled to the top of the rocks.
    "I want to go even higher!"
she announced, looking at an oak tree
growing on the bank. "Let's climb
to the top of that!"
    The friends raced off.
All except Murray, who
was beginning to worry.

"Oh dear," he sniffed.

Murray wanted to join in but his tummy felt very tight.

Then he remembered. "My box!" he said.

Quickly he scribbled down his thoughts.

I'm worried that Lara won't like me.

I'm worried that I'm not a very good climber.

I'm worried that everyone will laugh at me.

"Worries won't stop me!" he smiled, closing the box and trotting off to the tree.

MURRAY

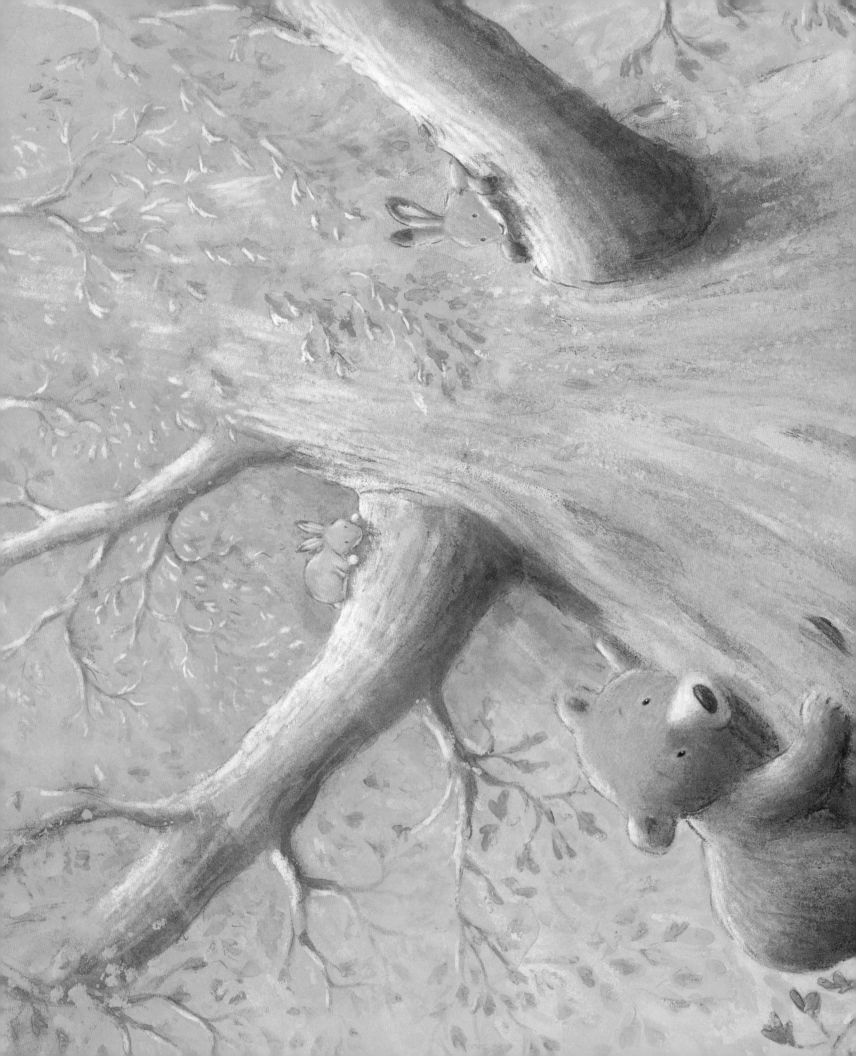

Up, up, up Murray climbed.

"Come higher!" called Lara. "You can see the sea!"

But Murray had spotted a hole in the trunk.

There, inside, was a nest of fluffy owl chicks!

"Look what I've found, Milly," he whispered.

All afternoon long, the friends played until it was time to go.
"Oh bother," Milly huffed, "I've lost my backpack."

Everyone hunted high and low till they found
the backpack hidden in the reeds.

"Just in time," said Alfie.
"The sun's starting to set."

"Hurry!" Lara squeaked in panic.
"We have to get home!"
   "Why? What's wrong?" asked Alfie.

Lara's whiskers quivered.

"We won't see where we're going!
 We'll be late for bedtime!
 And . . . and . . . I don't like the dark!"

Murray held Lara's paw. "Sharing worries makes
them feel smaller and less scary," he told her.
"See? I keep mine in a special box."
   He gave her a scrap of paper and a pencil.
"You can put yours in too," Murray smiled.

Lara stayed by Murray's side as they walked through the wood.

"Follow the fireflies," Murray said. "They're like nightlights to show us the path."

"Eeek!" Lara squeaked as an owl hooted overhead.

"It's OK," whispered Murray. "It's Mr Owl saying 'goodnight'." Across the treetops the friends heard a hoot in reply.

Soon they reached Alfie's house.
  "Just in time for bed," Alfie beamed.
  "Goodnight, everyone," said Lara.
"And thank you, Murray, for
being such a good friend."

High up on his thinking spot Murray and Milly looked out across the valley.

"Thanks for showing me the waterfall," said Murray.

"It wasn't too big or too loud?" asked Milly.

"It was both!" giggled Murray. "But it was also great FUN! I can't wait until we go again!"

More special stories to spark conversations . . .

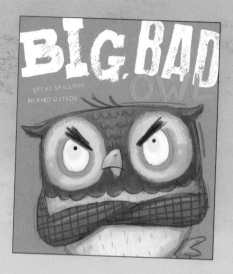

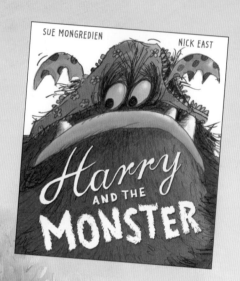

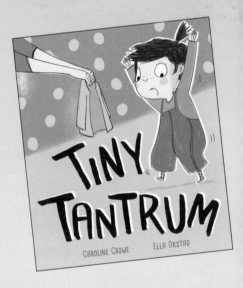

For information regarding any of the above titles or for our catalogue, please contact us:
Little Tiger Press Ltd, 1 Coda Studios,
189 Munster Road, London SW6 6AW
Tel: 020 7385 6333 • E-mail: contact@littletiger.co.uk
www.littletiger.co.uk